SWAN VANISHING

By Anna Tipton

Hidden Shelf Publishing House
P.O. Box 4168, McCall, ID 83638
www.hiddenshelfpublishinghouse.com

Artist: Megan Whitfield

Editor: Robert D. Gaines

Graphic Design: Rachel Wickstrom

Interior Layout: Kerstin Stokes

Library of Congress Cataloguing-in-Publication Data

Names: Tipton, Anna, author.
Title: Swan vanishing / Anna Tipton.
Description: McCall, ID: Hidden Shelf Publishing House, 2023.
Identifiers: ISBN: 978-1-955893-27-5 (paperback)
978-1-955893-28-2 (Kindle) | 978-1-955893-29-9 (epub)
Subjects: LCSH Swans--Fiction. | Shapeshifting--Fiction.
Ballets--Stories, plots, etc. | Fairy tales. | Romance fiction.
Love--Fiction. | BISAC FICTION / Magical Realism
FICTION / Fantasy / Romance
FICTION / Fairy Tales, Folk Tales, Legends & Mythology
Classification: LCC PS3620 .I78 S93 2023 | DDC 813.6--dc23

SMOKE

Light-winged Smoke! Icarian bird,
Melting thy pinions in thy upward flight;
Lark without song, and messenger of dawn,
Circling above the hamlets as thy nest;
Or else, departing dream, and shadowy form
Of midnight vision, gathering up thy skirts;
By night star-veiling, and by day
Darkening the light and blotting out the sun;
Go thou, my incense, upward from this hearth,
And ask the gods to pardon this clear flame.

– Henry David Thoreau

For Theo

1

It's almost time. I know because the last rays of sunlight are nearly gone, and I hear the swan call for me. A hush falls over the clearing, and the shadows of the wood move together like one organism. I wonder at the turning of the wind. Through my window I see the fortified walls of the kingdom rise against the velvety fabric of the sky. I shiver.

I make my way down the cold stone steps in the tower house, here on the lake outside the kingdom. I pause to watch blue-green lights flicker from my father's study. Drops of water slither down the limestone walls. I listen, imagining the dark work of his hands. Perhaps he's turning himself into a bird of prey for one of his nighttime roamings. Onward through the passageway, I fall into reverie. I lead with my head forward, neck and shoulders sunken like a vulture's.

The stairs take me into the entrance hall, and I hear an everlasting drip from my father's study above. On the ground in the cleavage of the stones, where the water pools, I see my reflection twisted with some sour thought. Today, I stop. Then, as if from some power in the water or the stones, my reflection changes, and instead of my face, I see the head of a swan.

Alarmed, I stomp on it. Soon the agitated water settles, and I see my own face once again.

I pull my mantle tightly around me and hurry on, heels clopping, through the hall.

Outside at last, I breathe deeply. I might have come from underwater, for inside the tower house the air is thick and dense. I creep like a lizard toward the lake, like a mouse scurrying through tall grasses and fog. Before me the ancient lake shivers with some secret thought. I stand in the stiff, solid wind, my flaxen hair almost silver in the moonlight.

At the lake I catch my breath. My cloak bellies in the wind. I feel the blood fighting through my limbs, and my gums flare from the cold. I'm the one who feels, a woman, not an animal nor a dream. I sigh in relief. The swan in the puddle was only a trick of the eye.

The bite of the wind calls me back to my purpose. I must check on Odette.

An ice wind rushes from the lake, and I shiver. I turn around, my breath the shape of white smoke. Dapples of light twinkle like tiny stars in the thousand dimples of the water's surface, and I see Odette, a pure white swan. I soften at her arrival. The moon emerges from behind a black cloud, like someone coming out of hiding, and the transformation happens in an instant. A bat screeches and flies out of a tree, stirred by this unnatural displacement. There was a swan, and now, standing in its place, is my twin sister Odette, her white cotton dress and hair luminous from the transformation.

2

Every night Odette turns into a woman, and every dawn she turns into a swan. She is beauty made and un-made every night. I'm the only one who sees her sorrow, and the only thing she can hope for is the impossible—for someone to love her and break her curse.

Together we listen to the gulping lake. In the distance golden balls of light bob in tandem with the waves. The kingdom and its concerns are far, far from us, and she and I pass the time like we're players in a double act between two great events of an age. This is waiting. We know it best. I wonder if anyone will set foot in our private kingdom of loneliness and anger. We have no reason to think that anything will change, that Father will give up his obsessions or that Odette will become free.

She says, "Does Father even care?"

"Maybe. I don't know."

"I can never fall in love."

"You could. It would be a disaster."

"Suppose someone found me." She breathes the chilly air. "And loved me."

"Suppose someone did."

"It would be my freedom."

I say nothing. If someone found her, he would take her away from me, and I would be truly alone.

In the distance comes the howling of coyotes, and I think of the cats climbing trees and hiding in garrets. Odette's teeth chatter, and I wrap my mantle around her. For now, while it is still dark, we have each other.

3

The good people of the kingdom know about my father and me—Odette they never see because of her enchantment. They're afraid of us because we perform magic, and so they keep away from this woodland outside their city walls.

Occasionally, though, a band of youth comes to devil us. Having made their way across the water, they climb out of their boat and stand on the bank taking in the dense forest, the tower house, and the craggy rocks that jut into the lake. We live in gloom and ruin, but it's my ruin. Our tower house has the look of a ceramic vase that's been broken and put back together. Ivy grows on the walls inside and out. Stones here and there have been pillaged from the walls. Birds nest in the corners of the roof. I love it. It was built for defense so one could watch and be unseen. That's what I've learned to do best, to watch and let no one know what's inside.

One of them says it would make a great place to hide

out, and I imagine them coming back here, their boat piled high with burgled goods.

Another youth points at me.

"Hey, you!"

I shouldn't have been too interested in them, leaning my head out the window. The boy has the audacity to begin climbing to my window, raising shouts at me with the others. The one who pointed throws a rock at me.

"Not again!" I mutter. I grab the nearest thing in sight—a clay pot—and drop it, nearly hitting the boy in the head. It shatters loudly on a rock. In a panic, the boy lets go and tumbles to the ground. The others scream at me. I haven't even cast a spell and they're terrified of me. They scurry into their boat and retreat across the water.

"Good riddance," I say and shut the window.

I suppose I encourage the rumors people spread about me. Even now I could do worse, setting fire to their pants or causing a leak in their boat. They think I'm dangerous. One guard claims he saw me shoot lightning bolts from my hands, and an old woman swears I stopped a vicious wolf from attacking me and sent it whimpering away.

Some of the rumors are true. I'm not proud of being magical. I never liked sorcery nor wanted it. The spark in my fingers scares me. Odette might be enchanted, but at least she can't help her situation. I feel as though I brought my magic on myself, and I'm ashamed every time I light a fire with my hand or cause the rain to fall. Sometimes I think if I tried hard enough, I could be like any other woman in the kingdom. Then when I walked through the market, the townsfolk might look at me and smile or maybe not look at me at all but let me pass, anonymous and unremarkable just like them.

Standing in the clearing and pursuing these pointless thoughts, I turn toward the house and shout, "What do you want with me?"

Water slops against the rocks. Starlings twitter in the trees, and a hawk plunges for an unwary rodent. From somewhere across the lake comes the clang of a hammer.

I blush at the shrillness of my voice. It's the first time I've spoken all day.

I grab a stick and slash the water.

Suddenly a flame blooms at the end of the stick. I jerk back and hurl it far away from me. A frog croaks and plops into the lake.

13

"I didn't mean to!" I cry. I make a face at my hands. "I didn't choose to be like this."

The swan floats on the lake and rests her patient eyes on me. I scowl at her. She accepts her enchantment so mutely, as a matter of course, as she would the aging of her body or the onset of winter. Nothing, not even her troubles, touches her grace. Sometimes I want to shake her.

I stomp off, leaving the grass swaying in my trail.

4

Although I'm not really welcome within the city walls, I have wished only the best for the royal family. Even now the king suffers from some deadly illness, and although they don't know it, I've helped him as much as I could, sneaking herbal remedies into his drinks and tempering his fevers. I wish I could do more.

Late one night the window of the king's sick chamber glows when all other lights have gone out. I can see it from across the lake. The prince and his mother must fear the worst, and I grab a potion and make my way toward the castle.

I cruise across the water like a dabbler, moving through moonbeams and starlight. Halfway across the lake I get the feeling I'm not alone. I squint through the violet-blue darkness and sense a disturbance in my wake, a human figure swimming underwater. I blink, but nothing surfaces. Shaking my head, I dip my oar in the water and row on.

My thoughts turn toward my father, Rothbart. I picture him in his study, brewing some nasty-tasting concoction. He's surrounded by animals, silent and still and covered with white cloth. He has made these sick or unwanted beasts his project, bringing them home and meaning to transform them into new creatures. Some of the creatures were sick or disabled, put aside to be killed. The pigs and chickens he stole from a farmer's dirty, cramped hutches. He found the fox and moose in the forest injured—from a hunting party, he suspected, judging from the tracks. Such is the carelessness of people. Now the animals are comatose, suspended in the twilight of enchantment, and he works tediously through his spell books.

He dwells on old memories as he hovers over his cauldron, the glow of the flame flashing across his raddled face. His study is a mess, with potions lying around, parchments and books heaped on the desk, and buckets and rags piling up in the sink. The great tragedy of his life was that my mother died in childbirth. I don't think he ever recovered from the loss, and perhaps he regrets bringing children into a world hostile toward magic. He likes me all right, but his moody silences make me wonder if I'm a painful reminder of happier days. If I asked him, he'd say he blamed himself for not saving my mother. Now he throws himself into hating the kingdom. Most of the time I wish he'd let go of his grudge, but sometimes, when he shakes with anger, cursing the palace guards under his breath, I find it in my heart to have compassion for him.

His obsessions became ingrown over the years. He used to turn into his hawk-like form and fly over the city, frightening the people with full-throated shouts, but over time his angst grew to an inward, sulking resentment. Now, instead of tormenting the kingdom folk, he turns to his projects. Every sick fox, every bird with a broken wing, every deer left to die, is a chance for him to reverse the forces of a cruel world.

It's all good and well for him to rescue animals, but it bothers me that he's cursed his own daughter to be a swan. The only answer I can think of, one that can't be reasoned with, is that in his warped thinking, Odette's curse is a form of justice.

He must be sparing her from something, a broken heart, perhaps, or the pain of being spurned. I wonder if he's sparing me, too. Once I looked up and his eyes were on me, searching me, trying to probe my thoughts.

"Odile, are you okay?" he asked suddenly, and his gentleness alarmed me. I didn't like it. I could understand his brusqueness, but his urgency worried me.

I said, "I'm okay. Are you?"

"Yes, I'm okay." His voice was low.

He wasn't always so concerned. At sixteen I had a fit of boldness. "Why did you do it?" I asked. I thought of the swan, my sister, who was about to turn into a woman again. She had been enchanted as long as I could remember.

I picked the wrong time to ask. He was in one of his sinister moods. At first his lips broke slowly into a smile, and then he pointed at me and laughed, his voice almighty but hollow. I knew he was holding something back. Maybe this was a big joke on me, or maybe he was crazy. My boldness evaporated, and I became aware of the evil smell in the room. I felt sick and fled, the echoes of his laughter filling the hall and pounding in my head.

There isn't much I can do to make him know my fury. My little acts of spite—putting his books out of order or peeling the labels off his jars on an idle afternoon— are lost on him.

Often, he would send me on one of his complicated errands, and I would see no point in it. Gather yarrow and nightshade from the forest. Drop an egg from the highest window of the tower house. I would fetch him fish live or burning nettle or some other strange ingredient, and he would take it thoughtfully, studying me as if he were gauging how much I understood.

Once I'm on my errands, I'm glad to be alone. I look at the lake and feel the deep churning inside of me, and I whisper, "What's the big secret?" Does my father see what I see? In puddles and in lake water, in mirrors and windows, in the shining eyes of my father's animals, and in my sister, that silent presence always near me—I am haunted by a face that doesn't seem like my own.

Still, I've grown used to my gloomy life on this outer rim. I'm grateful for the woodlands and the shadows which I love and the animals skittering at the sound of my footfalls. The soil knows me. When I trod down paths I've made with my own hands and feet, the earth clenches at my step. And in my heart I know I wouldn't be me if it weren't for my single-minded, shifting father or the grim thought that one day I might be like him.

Then, back from my errands, my father's cup stops fuming, and he questions me with his eyes. In his presence I feel as though my body is insubstantial, like vapor. I want to cry out to him, but in these massive stone walls where I can barely breathe the dense, wet air, where I flinch from the answers I do not wish to hear, my voice falls dead.

5

I try to leave these thoughts behind me as I make my way toward the castle and the king's sick chamber.

At the city gate I call, "Hey! Will you let me in?"

A guard on the wall looks at me and says something to another guard, and a third one joins them. They mutter to each other for some time.

I sigh. "Come on. What have I done?" My voice is so faint in the broad night they probably can't hear me.

A fourth guard joins them, and they continue watching me, talking among themselves. I imagine them pursing their lips with doubtful expressions. Their smugness galls me. They've made up their minds about me, and I want to know which rumor they've believed about me.

I leave them. I can get inside with or without their help, but now and then I hope for a little courtesy. People change. One never knows when someone's heart might soften or when some new guard on the job doesn't know any better than to help me. I walk along the wall and come in through a small, unguarded door that opens into a vegetable garden. A dog barks, and I make my way into the streets.

I prefer the city at night. In the heat of the day the smells of fish and skin and carcasses are more intense. Now, in the cool evening, the streets are quiet. The final stroke of the bell silenced bartering peddlers, gossiping neighbors, and the shrieks of children. The shops are closed, the windows shut. Baskets dangle from poles running along the buildings, and a breeze sends the baskets rocking. A cat climbs out of a window and slinks across a pole. It sees me and freezes.

I say, "Believe it or not, I want to help." The cat looks away and disappears into the night.

I approach the castle quickly, moving like instinct, almost as if I were flying. I intercept gardens and climb hedges. The guards are vigilant, but I'm stealthy. I've had years of sidestepping my father's eye. At last, on a ledge below the king's balcony, I stop and peer at the royal family through the balustrades. The king lies in bed, gray and sleeping. The queen sits reading in a chair next to him. Prince Siegfried stands on the balcony close to me. His jaw is set, and he looks straight across the lake where the unknown lies. The skin of his knuckles whitens as he clutches the railing.

Here where the king is beyond the help of natural healing, my bitterness melts like wax. I'm embarrassed at the pale power of my healer's hands, and I wish I were a true sorceress so I could help him even more.

Awkwardly keeping my balance on the ledge, I open my potion and let its fumes rise through the balustrades. I blow its soothing aroma in the direction of the king.

Siegfried's feet stir. He looks right at me, but, by some magic or trick of the eye, he doesn't see me. His brow relaxes. A page of the queen's book flutters, and she looks up and gazes at her son. The king sighs, his face a portrait of tranquility.

The breeze lifts, and Siegfried goes inside. His mother takes his hand, and together they look at their loved one.

Inside, I ache. I forget about Rothbart and his spite. I forget the guards and their hatred. None of that matters now. I wish I could cast a spell that would make the king rise out of bed, but I'm not strong enough.

I touch the wall one last time before I fly into the night.

6

I awaken in the boat, a bar of moonlight across my face. The sky is latticed with black foliage, and everything is touched by anguish.

Climbing out of the boat, I hear footsteps and see Odette coming out of the forest, her hair luminous like the water. She smiles and sits next to me. For a moment we listen to the crickets and the soft hooting of an owl. I think bitterly of the king and the brevity of life, and it pains me that Odette's life should be wasted because of her spell.

I say, "Why haven't you ever run away?"

"You know I can't. I'm bound by the spell."

"You don't know that. You've never tried."

"But then what could I do? I'm powerless in the day, Odile."

She isn't looking at me. She's looking at the lights in

a faraway tower, and suddenly her beauty makes me depressed. I dread the day when someone will find her and give her a brighter future.

I lower my head. "At least your life would be yours."

7

Not long after, the king passes. My medicine was less than healing, and sleep was pale relief, the drifting ever closer to the veil. Where I want to bind together, the reeds pull apart. Where I want to offer something rich and hot, the doors are shut, and always, at night, Odette's glittering eyes meet mine. I feel at once sympathy and guilt. No amount of sorcery can deaden the pain of loss and loneliness, and we might carry out the rest of our days like this, doubting ourselves and wishing for something to happen, while beyond the lake kings rise and fall like cycles of rainwater.

8

Early in the day I go into town to pick up some bread and candles. My hood is low over my face. Though the people shift their weight and look at the ground when I visit their shops on the market street, they don't mind me when I pay for their goods.

The streets are hot and grimy. A cart creaks as it passes by. A peddler follows me trying to hold a mirror to my face. She's either too blind to realize who I am or too eager to turn a penny. I brush past her, coughing in the dusty air.

She follows me, and children run by me screaming.

I stop and squint at the sky, barely able to see for the dust and sweat. I can't remember how late it is, and I dread the long walk home.

I become aware of a mirror in my hand. The peddler, who won't take a hint, put it there, rambling about the wonders of being young. I blink at myself in the glaring sun, and to my horror I watch my reflection in the mirror move of its own accord. I see a child playing hide-and-seek in the castle, darting in and out of the shadows. The child becomes a woman who pounds on the city gates. Now she's a sorceress, searching for her way through a fog. Then I see Odette, whose eyes are charged with a new magic.

I shove the mirror back into the peddler's hands and hurry away.

9

Though the illusions from the mirror trouble me, I shake them off on my way home. Illusions are deceiving, I tell myself. Mirrors only show what's on the outside.

I step off the causeway. As I make my way through the ferns, I sense the place is different. The lake is still and flat like glass. I listen but do not hear the usual chorus of crickets. A wind courses through the ferns, and my skin crawls with gooseflesh. I look behind me, but no one's watching.

The distant sound of voices comes to me, so strange in this remote place. I strain my ears. Then I hear laughter.

Creeping closer, I squint though the foliage, pushing the shrubs out of the way, and discern two figures.

Odette sits on the bank of the lake in earnest conversation with Prince Siegfried, of all people. I steady myself against a tree, baffled. Then I climb the branches, my sack of goods bouncing at my side, and peer at them.

I can't hear what they're saying—what he's saying, for Odette listens as silent as an oak. I stare at them, trying to piece together how this happened. Maybe, considering the king's death, it isn't too far-fetched after all. Siegfried, scarred by the loss of his father, losing sense of time and place, ventured deeper into the forest than ever before. After the sun had set, he came upon a woman he had never seen, so different from the noblewomen he knew at court. She might have bewitched him at once, and I imagine him wordlessly laying his crossbow aside.

As for Odette, a new impression blooms on her face. Slowly, she smiles, and I see a spell taking hold of her, one that couldn't be called forth by the words of a sorcerer.

Odette and I both know that if a man vows his love for her, her curse will be broken. I watch her swear silently to herself, in that dreamy landscape behind her lips where no one will hear. She will leave the lake forever and never look back.

My sack slides off my shoulder. I catch it before it crashes to the ground, and then I lower myself down.

A candle falls out of my sack and rolls into the bushes, but I leave it, stumbling toward the tower house. I recall Odette's dream that someone would find her. I want her to be free, but not this way, not by the love of the prince. He doesn't understand us, and she would never fit in with his kind.

I cover the distance to the house, breathless, and scramble up the stairs. Inside my chamber I hurry to the window to look at them again, convincing myself I'm not making this up. They're still talking, smiling at each other, and I raise my eyes to the silent, shifting woodland beyond.

He's going to take her away from me, and I see our life, my sister's and mine, cease to be what we have always known.

I turn away from the window. Like an animal I crawl into my corner where I sleep, bewildered, away from the moonlight.

10

So, Odette is found.

Pacing in my chamber, I let the thought sink in. I blink and imagine what it would be like for my own life to take a course of its own. I think of shy blossoms, showing their faces only at night. I want to shout, "What about me?" Between their hushed words and occasional glances at the tower house, Odette probably forgot I was here, too, watching for the first rays of morning.

I can't accept his love as the answer to Odette's waiting. He will never truly know her. Their histories are too different. He could never plumb the depths of her curse or understand the shadow that comes with her—me, her crotchety twin sister. Love's word might break her spell in body, but it couldn't heal her from the sorrow that touched her soul. No soft word could wake her from the daymare she's lived all her life.

I see the future in Odette's face and know she will follow him out of these woods. I pause at the window and stare at the large clouds gathering in. I will be here at the lake, as I always have been, to watch her take on a life that isn't mine.

I walk over to the washstand and splash my face with cold water. Again, I see my reflection warp and change into a swan, fragmented by the agitated water.

"Stop it!"

I hurl the water out the window, and a raven shrieks and flaps away.

11

It's been days since I've spoken to Odette. When I do at last, I find her walking down a wooden path.

She says, "Odile, I've been found."

"I know."

I fall into step with her, folding my arms and looking at the trees.

Odette continues, "This will change everything. He can break my curse!"

I consider her. She's excited for her freedom and blushing with spring love. One word only and the spell would be finished. Then she'd embrace her royal family as her own. She's becoming her own person, having experiences I can't share, and it makes me jealous. All I can do is watch from afar or sulk in my chamber.

I feel sick at the thought. "So. If he promises to love you?"

"I'll be free."

"You'll be free."

"Yes."

Hogwash.

"When he speaks to me, Odile, I lose all sense of time—I don't even know how long he stayed that first night. He must have gone back before sunrise because he didn't see me change back into a swan."

She forgets herself, talking to me like this. She might have been singing to the birds. I would have been fascinated by this second enchantment, one brought on by love, if it didn't make me so cross.

"I told him about my curse, but he didn't run away. He seemed to care even more for me. He asked me all these questions, and sometimes we just listened to the woods together, and I felt him looking at me. I could have told him about the frightening things Father could do. I could have scared him away by telling him the magic I've seen. Or worse."

I wait for her to go on, but she doesn't. I say quietly, "That you were a sorceress?"

She nods. "Suppose I did. He would never want to see me again."

"We'd be better off for it. He would be, too."

"I know you would have wanted me to stay hidden,

but I didn't want to scare him off or make myself seem worse than I am."

I look away.

"Oh, Odile. I didn't mean it like that. You know you can't help yourself." She touches my shoulder, but I say nothing. "If he loves me—and I think he does—then I'm not going to hide from him. He's going to keep coming to see me."

A mean part of me wishes I had intercepted Prince Siegfried before he found her. If only I had been there to stop this.

I say. "If you were yourself around him, he'd never come back. He's too afraid to know what you'd really say. It would make him uncomfortable."

I'm grasping at any reason to make her abandon her fancies, making the prince seem worse than he probably is. What do I know about men? Only what I've observed in the kingdom, the way they tend to talk more than listen and don't include women in important conversations. The prince is a good man, but I'm bothered by the thought that he would free her. She would owe him her life, and who knows how the court would use that to try to control her?

There's also the matter of people's opinions about

us. They'd learn about her curse and hate her. If Siegfried's vow fell through and she was stuck being a swan, they'd want to get rid of her, purging the land of such unnaturalness. They might be no match for Rothbart, but they could easily drive out a vulnerable and speechless swan-woman.

"I'm telling you." I'm babbling now, jealous—or afraid. I can see from her expression that I'm hurting her. "You'll get to know each other, and then you'll see he just talks over you. You could tell him how lousy it is being a swan and that you hate your spell, and he'd wait for you to finish so he could tell you his own thoughts about it."

Odette smiles and shakes her head. "I don't think you understand love, Odile. What's so wrong with needing his help? I want him to help me. I want to always put him before me. That's my dream now. My whole life has been building up for this. If only you knew what it felt like right before I turned into a woman. It hurts, but it's also one of the best feelings because the worst is almost over. I think it's a taste of what's about to come, the joy of breaking out of that horrible body forever." She beams at the path ahead of us. "You know, I think I was meant to be cursed just so I could be loved by him."

I stare at her, wondering where she picked up such codswallop. Certainly not from me. There's no arguing with her when she's like this.

I wonder how the night would have turned out differently if Siegfried had found me instead of Odette. He would know I was the sorceress by my mantle, the peevish look on my face, and something else, a stirring in the air around us. He's been warned about me, and I'm sure the sight of me would correspond to the dismal descriptions of his counselors. He would have fled deeper into the forest, perhaps beyond the point of no return, or he would have seized this opportunity to encounter the menace of the lake, raising his crossbow at me, his grief giving him new daring.

I study Odette and wonder at our shared beauty. How is it that even though we're identical, her presence is bright and inviting? I feel that old shame again, the darkness that makes me different from her. I let it hang in the air between us.

She says, "I know it makes you sad. You think I won't need you anymore." She pauses thoughtfully. "We don't understand magic, but we'd be fools if we didn't lay hold of our moment when it arrived—even if it wasn't what we expected or wanted. We're just cut-paper shadows compared to what we might become. We seem free like birds in these woods, but inside we're bound by our demons. You know that, Odile."

We come to a clearing by the lake and sit down on some boulders.

She goes on. "Rothbart's magic was found by those who wanted to control other people, but it doesn't have to be used that way, Odile. You don't need to hide from it. You could bring good and healing to this realm. You already did when you helped the king as much as you could."

I harumph.

"You did help him," she insists. "His end was out of your control. You can't stop death, Odile, no matter what Father thinks."

The trees creak and sough in the breeze. Odette shakes her head thoughtfully and says, "One day, it will be your freedom, not mine, that will center us."

I could snap at her for speaking with so much confidence in her hopes. Controlling myself, I say, "I don't think you feel the enchantment the same as I do. You have the chance to be different now, but I never will be."

We sit in silence for some time. She'll do what she wants, and I'll turn toward my sorcery, my only resort. I feel us growing deeper in our ways like reeds bent in opposite directions.

"It's day now," I say, pointlessly, for she sees the glowing horizon, too.

She rises and steps into the water.

A panic comes over me now that she's left my side. Alone on the bank, no longer hearing her steady breathing, I'm almost afraid of myself, afraid certainly of what I'd do left to my own devices, without her presence guiding me.

Only this I know: before there was a woman, and now there's a swan.

12

Days pass, and I begin to see Odette the swan everywhere—the long, sloping neck; the silent beak; the round, onyx-black eye. I see her in the puddle at the bottom of the stairs. She is in the lake and the sky, hiding by day in the clouds and at night in the sparkling stars of Cygnus.

As Prince Siegfried continues to visit Odette, I feel more and more like a passing breath, a shadow. When I should feel happy, I feel gloomy. When I should feel nothing, focusing on whatever task at hand—washing clothes or gathering mushrooms—I feel a jolt. The change taking place in Odette causes a change in me, and I find myself reaching for my father's spell books.

One day I go into his study, that pentagon of choking smells and stinging smoke. He's gone out. Bottles roll around the floor, and rags lie on the counter, dry and sculptural. Some viscous fluid drips from its bottle onto the floor. My father's animals lie covered and stiff against the wall. I lift one of the white cloths and start when I find a black swan underneath.

I reach out to touch her wing, and suddenly, automatically, like a machine, she turns her eye on me, glassy and unseeing.

I cover her up quickly and shudder in the eerie, dim light. I put my hands on my cheeks, human, but inside I don't feel like myself.

I hear Rothbart's footfalls coming from the corridor. Quickly, not wanting to be seen, I grab a spare sheet, shake it out, and let it fall over me, hiding my head and figure. Now, covered and shapeless, my back against the wall, I stare through the fibers, my eyes algae green.

13

I try to get used to the idea of Odette living in the castle, but I'm convinced she'll never fit in. I imagine her sharing dinner with his family and the court, and Odette, feral lake-woman that she is, sitting tense before all these strange people, probably offending them with her crude table manners. The queen, smiling sweetly, all graciousness, offers her a plate of quail.

Odette looks at her shyly and says, "No, thank you. I don't eat meat."

A hush falls over the table. Beside her Siegfried slowly lowers his goblet.

"Then you won't have your strength," the queen says decidedly. Those who know her would hear the annoyance in her tone.

Odette pales. She looks at Siegfried, who's studying the pattern on his goblet. Around the table the juices of viands ooze on the plates of friends and counselors. The queen is still standing there offering Odette the quail.

Then, pretending to be clueless, Odette blinks dumbly at the queen. That august woman suddenly laughs and says there's plenty else to eat. When she returns to her seat, though, she looks at Odette with a new expression. This was the woman who would lead her people? If she could not eat with them, she could not live with them.

14

One night I sneak up to the palace and overhear Siegfried and his friend Benno in a courtyard. I bend around a pillar and see His Highness sitting on a stone bench, grimacing and scratching his ankles.

Benno leans on a giant planter, his arms folded, frowning at the prince. He can't stand it any longer. "Won't you stop? You're going to draw blood."

"Benno, you wouldn't believe the bugs down there! I don't know how she isn't eaten alive."

"Well, she is a creature herself, as you say." I can tell from Benno's tone that he doesn't like Odette. "Do you really think she can be queen?" He watches Siegfried carefully.

"I know she can."

"You're drawing blood now."

Siegfried holds his fingers up and sees blood. He wipes it away and puts his boots back on.

"I just don't think it's a good idea," Benno says. "I've been reading several bestiaries, and I don't think she's as harmless as you think."

Siegfried stands and touches him lightly on the shoulder. "You read too much about sorcery, Benno." "We have a sorcerer on our hands, Your Highness, and one of the ways we can protect ourselves is by studying his ways."

"Have you ever met him? Maybe he's not so bad." The prince breathes the fresh night air and starts walking in my direction. I panic and skirt around to the other end of the pillar.

"The stars tonight, Benno! Look, there's Cygnus. I can't wait for everyone to meet her."

Benno murmurs, "I mean this kindly, Your Highness, but you are being courted by delusion. I'm worried for our people, your people. You don't know what you're letting in with this woman."

Siegfried stands at the viewpoint overlooking the city streets. His gaze falls on a gargoyle pulling a frightful face. He studies it thoughtfully, and a cloud forms over his features. Benno stands quietly beside him, and together they listen to the final strokes of the bell and watch the people slowly desert the streets.

15

Prince Siegfried comes to Odette like weariness, like a wanderer in search of a place to rest, clambering over hedges and broken trees. He comes like the plague.

I decide he loves her because she's enchanted, and that makes her unlike any other woman in the world. Though he wouldn't admit this, perhaps he feels good about himself for saving her from misfortune. Odette forgets herself as she listens to every word he says. I know her. She thinks the best of people and would never believe a man of such kindness would love her for a spell.

He begs her to come to the castle, where she would be safe and looked after and have a proper room to live in, but she shakes her head. "Not yet. You are on my father's land." She nods at the tower house. "He could harm us if he wanted to."

So for now he settles to meet her at the lake until the

right moment comes for her to leave.

When he's not talking about plans for the kingdom, he tells her stories, fantastic tales about apples that poison the flesh and kisses that heal it, about villains who get what they deserve and good people who live long after the story ends. He speaks quietly, his voice a steady murmuring of words, as calm as the gentle waves of the lake.

I see us in his tales. Odette gets the prince, her reward for her patient suffering, and Odile the sorceress gets a lifetime of loneliness, her due for having power like her father.

His stories are as true as magic, as passion—as this, when he lays his hand softly, for the first time, on hers. I tell myself it can't be real, and yet I'm moved by his earnestness. I wish I were in Odette's place, and the words he said to her were spoken to me.

I trudge back to the tower house. I fear Odette would be miserable in the castle. Every day something would make her embarrassed of her low, wild station. She wouldn't want them to do her hair up like lavish cake frosting on special occasions or paint red powder on her cheeks. She is a different kind of creature. Above all I fear she would forget about me, never returning to this outer rim she came from, the place where she left loneliness and unfeeling darkness behind. I would be left creeping around in the woodland, groping in the gap between consciousness and death, that old twilight that makes everything grey. I shiver in the dusky night.

"Why shouldn't she become queen?" I mumble to myself, walking aimlessly through the dark. "If I stood in the way, what does that make me?"

I look back at them, doubting he would ever understand the anguish of Odette's enchanted years. She keeps it to herself, not wanting to trouble him. Maybe her spell makes him feel like her protector. With her doe-eyes on him, he could slay a dragon. He might even look forward to his people's praise. They would admire him for lifting a broken woman from the hand of a sorcerer.

I make my way back to my chamber, my mind a whirlpool. When I dip my hands in the water basin, I see the face of a swan looking back at me. I don't fling it away this time but return its gaze steadily. Upstairs the old man coughs. I imagine him flipping through spell books, searching for a way to resurrect all dead things from the earth.

I lie down and listen to the dry reeds rustling in the wind. Before long I sleep.

16

Not long after this, Rothbart appears to them. The night rings with the noise of cicadas. From behind my boulder I hear his footsteps and a splash of some creature diving for its life.

Prince Siegfried hears him coming, too. He springs to his feet, believing, instinctively, that whatever comes from these woods must be a threat. Like a soldier ready to attack at the sudden hour, he pulls out a knife. "Who's there?"

Odette covers her face with her hands. "No, please."

The moon dims, and I become aware that the cicadas are silent.

Then we hear Rothbart's labored breathing. His footfalls are heavy, and Prince Siegfried, when he sees his dark form, solid as a boundary stone, lowers his knife.

I glance at Siegfried. From what I can tell in the darkness, his skin is white, as white as Odette's cotton dress. He is silent and watchful, rigid as a hound about to charge.

"Can't you leave us alone?" Odette moans.

Rothbart's voice is hoarse. "I will say only this." Yesterday I would have thought there was anger in his tone, but tonight I hear the weariness, deep to the bone. He says to Odette, "You might think this boy's love is going to make your life better." Rothbart looks at me. A twig snaps loudly under my feet, and I freeze like a deer sensing a predator. "But you're not who you think you are, and sooner or later you're going to have to look squarely at yourself in the mirror."

Odette folds her arms and refuses to look at him. Siegfried looks from Rothbart to my sister and back. My face is hot with embarrassment. I don't know what he meant, but I sense that his words have everything to do with my sister and me.

Rothbart doesn't linger. When he's gone, Odette relaxes. Siegfried puts his arm around her, and they speak comfortingly to each other.

After a while Siegfried leaves us in the darkness. Odette sits in the moonlight with her eyes on the lake, and I sit crouching with my back against the boulder, my heart pounding. Slowly we breathe more easily, and little by little the cicadas sound up again.

17

I keep thinking about my father's words, his challenge for Odette—or for me to face myself in the mirror. Once, looking at my reflection in the lake, I imagine it's not a reflection at all but Odette staring back at me from the other side of the water. Her eyes are wide with terror, and she's reaching for me. I could pull her out if I wanted to, but instead I look away.

18

One warm summer's eve, on the prince's birthday party, I come to the castle stealthily, not wanting to be seen. In the ballroom, the scent of the forest is on me, the smell of pine and late-fallen leaves. It's the smell, I realize, of Odette, so different from the perfumes wafting through the hall.

My shadow falls across the wall in the shape of a swan. I stop and wonder at it.

"It's only an illusion," I whisper.

I shake my nerves off and make my way into the ballroom. Prince Siegfried stands at the end of the room, silent and thoughtful. There's a starved look in his eye, and I wonder if he's taken to heart Benno's warning about the dangers of Odette.

The room is full of people dancing. Soon Siegfried will become king, and his mother wants him to find a bride by then. The queen stands next to her son, smiling at the noblewomen and tapping her finger to the tempo.

I perch myself on a railing and lose interest in the dancing women. They're too careful, thinking about their steps, consciously trying not to mess up. Their footwork never mattered as much as it does tonight, so they think. They find the culmination of their life's training in the point of their feet before the prince.

I creep to a statue of a woman holding a vase and peer through the crook of her arm. The queen talks to Siegfried about her plans for his bride, speaking of this woman as a special possession to show off to neighboring kingdoms, and it makes me angry. Has she learned nothing from her own years of service?

Siegfried tells her he's found the woman he wants to marry. She smiles at this news. He says this woman is a revelation. He's a new man. He wouldn't consider anyone else.

I force myself not to cringe. His mother raises her cup to this lucky woman. Her eyes are bright with a vision of their domain expanding, her son at the helm and this young queen at his side.

"Who is she?" She scans the room looking from one woman to the next.

He hesitates. "She isn't here tonight, Mother, but she'll be ready to meet you soon."

His eyes lock on mine. I blanch. The music swells as the dance quickens, and his mother tugs at his sleeve, trying to get his attention. But Siegfried stares at me, his face framed by the statue's triangular arm.

He gestures at me. I crawl into the open cautiously, my heart pounding. I expect him to greet me, mistaking me for Odette, but he doesn't. He hardly even acknowledges me. I sense some old magic at work, swirling around me like a vortex.

Suddenly I realize that Siegfried doesn't see me at all. The illusion has come back, for now, instead of a woman, he sees a swan. He's surprised to see one at such a crowded event and gestures to draw his mother's attention toward me. I try to speak, but I have no mouth. I want to cover my face in my hands, but I have no hands to hide behind. My neck feels infinite. I stretch it out and almost knock the queen's cup out of her hand. Then, struck by the ridiculousness of it, I laugh, an animal squawk.

What nightmare am I living in? I think of my father poring over his diagrams, taking notes, suddenly looking up at me. I think of his hints that Odette isn't who she thinks she is and my inkling that Odette's curse is mine, too. I hear him muttering to the empty darkness around him: *One day you'll look at yourself in the mirror and not recognize yourself.*

Everyone who has been near me knows that I'm different. It's the reason people are uncomfortable around me, why they breathe more easily when I'm gone. Perhaps it's also the reason Prince Siegfried comes to see Odette only at night. He wouldn't know what to do if he saw her as a swan, and the magic of her daytime form disturbs him like the magic of my sorcery.

I want to charge headlong into the dancing ladies, shrieking, wings flapping, trying to force sense back into my being. It dawns on me that I feel the same pressure these women feel—the anxiety to be pleasing and the desperation to cover myself up with prettiness. I'm mortified by this swan body. My inner ravings are physical and laid bare for all to see.

His mother gawks at me. "A swan!"

Breathing quickly, wordless, I throw my head back and shriek.

Siegfried runs at me, waving his arms to shoo me away, but by now I'm high in the air, soaring through the night like an arrow, my mind bent on one purpose: to get away.

19

I don't know how long it takes to get back to the tower.

My knees shudder. The illusion is over now, and I'm a woman again. I look at the lake from my window and see Odette. Wading, she feels the cool water lap her shins and loses herself in her dreams. I have always believed in her substance, but tonight as I watch her, eyes stinging with tears, I feel like I'm watching myself.

I crawl into my bed like an animal, away from the moonlight, bewildered, covering my face.

20

I decide it's time to confront my father for answers.

At the door to his study, I make myself soundless. I grip the door handle but do not turn it, losing resolution all of a sudden. A part of me doesn't want to know what's going on with these visions. It would be easier to cling to the ignorance I've known all along.

He senses me before I can change my mind.

"It's all right, Odile. You can come in."

I step inside and hang by the door, feeling childish and shy and fingering the hem of my sleeve. I imagine the objects around the room imbued with special power: a precious stone, bottles of white powder, a basket woven with an intricate pattern, a collection of beetles pinned inside a frame. My eyes fall on a book open to a diagram of a swan with strange characters written all over its body.

My father stands over several jars of cultures. He

holds one to the firelight and gives it a gentle shake. Inside, the brown tendrils swirl.

"So," he says.

I stare at him, uneasy. The peat fire rages in the hearth, and in the backlight I can't make out his features very well.

"You're wondering what will happen to Odette."

I'm relieved I don't have to bring it up. I hate how thin my voice sounds in this room.

"You must already know this," he says, lowering the jar, "but her spell's going to break if Prince Siegfried vows to love her."

I relax a little and stop fussing with my sleeve. This is one of those rare moments when my father is candid with me, and I wonder if he was thinking about Mother just now. Though he's a hard man, the gentleness in his voice reminds me he loves me as best he knows how.

"You've been sensing other things, too, haven't you?" He looks at me. "Bird shadows, swan faces everywhere, a strange connection to Odette? Sometimes when people look at you, you think they see a swan."

I nod.

"I meant what I said when I told Odette she isn't who

she thinks she is. The prince has found her, and the day has come for you to look at yourself in the mirror."

I study the swan diagram. As his speech runs over me, I feel less and less myself and more like Odette, animal and dumb. My sister's likeness, her strange metamorphosis, her light to my dark—all occur to me as I take in his words.

He says, "Odile, this won't be easy for you to hear, but the person you believe is your sister is you."

I feel the coldness of the stone floor through the soles of my shoes. Steady drips of water, insistent and loud in that cavernous room, fall from some leaky corner into an earthenware jar. I fix my mind on that sound. The space between my father and me seems to lengthen and lengthen. It's as if his words come to me from across the lake.

Rothbart begins to pace, restless, and an edge creeps into his voice. "I didn't mean for this to happen. When I put the curse on you, I was trying to protect you from getting hurt. I knew people would persecute you because you were my daughter. They would despise you because you were magical."

He stops and stares at the space in front of him, as if he could see them charging at me in his mind's eye.

"I tried to hide you. I made it so that you were a swan in the daytime, and I gave you special abilities so you could be swift like a bird. I thought you would be safer that way, at least until you could handle sorcery on your own. Then you'd be able to protect yourself." He sighs heavily. "The spell didn't go as I had planned. There seem to be two of you now, and only the phantom part of you turns into the swan by day. I've tried, but there's nothing I can do to reverse the spell."

I put my hand on the wall to steady myself. Each phrase he utters resounds through my chest like the ringing of the town bell. He made me believe I had a twin sister who shared in my misery. I recall him pointing at me and laughing when I asked him why he cursed Odette. He never answered my question, and now I know why. He was pointing at me. I think of the visions I saw in the peddler's mirror, one lost woman following another. Now I see that Odette's ravings are my ravings, and her curse is mine.

21

I stand motionless, feeling the pulse growing stronger in my fingers. Outside, the swan steps onto the lake, sending ripples across the smooth waters. Maybe all along she was only pretending to be mute, bottling the silent scream inside of me.

"But she's my sister," I say, finding my voice at last. "She's always been with me. Who have I been talking to all this time? Who has the prince been meeting every night?"

"I knew this would be difficult for you," Rothbart says. "It seems the prince has been sharing the dream with you."

"Why did you do it?" My voice rises. I'm nearly shouting. "You made me think I had a sister. I feel trapped here because of you."

He doesn't meet my eyes. Though I know his words must be true, I still believe Odette is at the lake, as here as ever.

Rothbart shrugs. "It was a side effect or a spell gone wrong. I don't understand magic. I'm just a spell-caster. For a while, it will still seem like you have a sister. I'm sorry, Odile. I didn't want this for you."

He truly is sorry. I sense it in the strain of each sentence. It isn't easy for him to admit his mistake. I let him sit in his regret for a moment.

"What do I do?" I say.

His brow softens, and his voice lifts, hopeful. "There's a way to set it right, but it won't be easy. The curse will break if you take her place when the prince vows to love her."

"What do you mean?"

"If he believes that you're Odette when he says the magic words, your spell will break."

"But what will happen to Odette?"

He looks at me for a long moment. "You won't be seeing anymore of Odette after that."

22

I leave him to brood over his jars. Once I'm in the corridor, I stagger and lean against the wall. A spider backs away into a crevice.

I wipe the tears off my face, hands shaking, and continue walking down the corridor. The life I knew, the one I shared with Odette, vanished today like the snuffing of a candle. I walk quickly, nearly running, hardly knowing where I'm going. My father's words play over and over in my mind like an incantation: *You won't be seeing anymore of Odette after that.* Am I then to displace my sister? Maybe I'm wicked for turning on Odette, for finding a way to end her life so that I can have my own. Odette said once there may be a way for me to use sorcery to heal rather than harm. How little did she know her words would come back to wound her!

I descend the stairs and make my way across the foyer. A rat scampers out of my way. I shove the heavy front door open and let myself outside. Shivering, I hear the far-off toll of the bell. The larks warble in the trees.

23

One thing I have never regretted. My father's spell made my sister my own. I was the only person she had. We needed each other. She was me.

And she is me.

Rothbart was right. I continue to see her as if she were a separate self. I don't tell her about it. She carries on unreflectingly as if we were sisters. Perhaps I'm not ready to let her go, to embrace the deep quiet I fear will come once she's gone. When I pleaded with her once to let this romance with the prince fall away, I might have been reasoning with myself, a part of me that wanted Siegfried to be my own. Perhaps all along I've been at odds with that dreamy part of me that believed a prince would make my life all right.

Now when I watch Siegfried and Odette, studying my phantom sister with an elevated vision, I sense that Odette is an image of myself untouched by sorcery, a better version of me that is obedient to the voices around her.

Siegfried says to her, "Come to the ball, Odette. Please. My mother wants me to announce my bride. I will make my vow then."

Odette leans into his words as if they were an incantation. "Your vow," she echoes.

In her mouth that word is more than a word—her whole enchanted, captive soul cries out for it. In that word she gives herself over to him with the same focus I have when I cause the rain to fall. I'm afraid I'm about to scream. Siegfried's intention rouses the animal hatred inside of me, and I want to quell the destiny of this word with my hands. Odette sits there, innocent like runaway drops of water on a slick stone.

They watch a shooting star blaze across the night sky. When it vanishes, her hand is in his.

I wither inside. I'm caught between my frustration at her for being borne away by her fancies and the horror that I would steal these fancies from her. In a flash I see the person I might have been if my bitterness had never taken root.

Immediately I hate the thing that I am.

She says to him, "I promise I'll come."

She makes her promise with the gentleness of a dove. Her breath is the freshness of the night, and he holds her hand as if it were a fragile treasure. Her devotion is like magic to him. He watches her, moved as if he's seen a revelation. She is no ordinary woman, and she opened his eyes to the dewy earth at ease, the shifting cattails, the secretive ash and cottonwood. He didn't know the world out here existed or that he, too, could be a creature of the night, in and for it, rather than a lord contending with it.

Odette is the future of his kingdom. He would drink the pure lake water, smell the faint notes of pine, rub his hands on the velvety moss. When he came that first night, running from his sorrow, perhaps also scoping out the rugged woodscapes where he might expand his domain, Odette came, too, eclipsing the sparkle in his eyes, and put forward a greater reality, one which seized him body and soul.

He would bring back the woman who had been lost. It was crazy. It was the most perfect thing.

But what would happen to me? She is not hers to give.

I want to charge at him and push him into the lake, letting the ice-cold water pop the bubble of his fantasy. I would shout, "Go shoot your crossbow or whatever it is you do. Leave us alone." Then I would make Odette look at me. "Don't you know who you are?"

But I remain crouching in the shadows. That choking is the sound of my sobbing.

Presently it starts to shower. At my feet the leaves go up in small flames. I watch the fire flare in the quenching rain.

24

Another night Benno comes with Prince Siegfried to see Odette. He comes with a great crossbow and a measured expression. He can't be fooled, not even in these woods with phantom paths and marshy clearings. He watches his step as if looking for a quagmire or a trap, scrunching his nose in concentration as he hops over a tricky ridge.

I lean out my window and hear the sudden shuffle of critters as they dash into hiding. The cattails shudder, releasing fuzzy seeds into the wind.

The two men are pleased to get away from the court and breathe the green air of the forest. I wait for it to work on them like a potion, but when I see the crossbow, I can't help my annoyance.

"We're not out to get you," I whisper.

The lovers sit and talk, and Benno prowls around the lake like a predatory cat, alert, sidestepping mud puddles. He might have never been afraid until this moment, never truly prepared to shoot something. He glances at the prince now and then and squats and touches the earth. He holds his thoughts close to himself, saving them, I suppose, until he's alone with the prince and can speak more freely. His face softens when Odette addresses him. He shapes his expression so she can't read him. A raccoon steps out of the trees and paws a piece of bark, eyeing Benno darkly as if it understood he was no friend to the woods.

Sometimes Siegfried's face breaks into a grin, one that's youthful and carefree, and I imagine him as he was before his father took a turn for the worse.

He's still smiling when Benno says suddenly, watching Odette, "We have to leave, Your Highness."

But Siegfried is engrossed in conversation with Odette. We all knew the moment would come when they would have to go, but now that it's here, it's as if the prince never really believed Odette would turn into a swan.

Again Benno says, "Your Highness."

Siegfried's smile fades, and he looks at Odette for a long moment. She returns his gaze with fear in her eyes. Though she won't go with him yet, she questions him with her eyes. *Must I do this again, and every morning, until the ball?* Here before her daily sorrow, she's like a wounded animal. The quietness and contentment she feels when she's with him fall away before the reality of her curse.

The prince follows Benno out of the clearing, but not before one last look, just as she collapses into the water, a swan.

25

Beneath the surface of my soreness and envy, I feel a stirring, deep as the lake, of hopelessness.

I lay my cheek on one of my books, hoping to hear voices from the other side of the cover tell me I didn't need to ruin Odette. Sometimes, still half believing she's really here, I want to run to her and tell her I was wrong. I would tell her Siegfried is the greatest thing that happened to her. Her love is deep and wide because she doesn't think of herself as his equal. I would say all this if only we could be friends again. Her love for Siegfried would be nothing to me so long as we could go back to the way we were before.

I would say to her, "Don't be afraid! You have a prince who loves you, who gives you hope. You are his."

Yet I betray myself if I let Odette have her fantasy. She thinks she's saving herself, but she isn't. She's stepping from one entrapment to another. Surrounded by lords and ladies of a different league, she'll be more alone than she is here. The prince thinks he's making a heaven for himself in taking her for his bride, but he doesn't realize I'm coming to haunt his ball.

I open a book wearily and blink at the strange characters. As if the turmoil in my chest gives me a newfound grip on my powers, I begin to comprehend the words.

The dread of Siegfried's love and Odette's self-deception light a purpose for my task. Whatever it would mean for her, I must seize my life.

26

Late one night Odette brings Rothbart a bowl of grains and a flask of wine. She pauses when she sees me hard at work over Father's spell books. With a quick intake of breath, she looks at me as if something's dawned on her. She's upright and queenly, and the very light in the room seems to come from her. Hunched at my desk, I feel as ugly as a rat.

"Odile," she says, her syllables delicate like drops of water. I expect her to be frosty toward me for taking my magic seriously, but in those syllables I sense her heart reaching out to mine. I feel the meaning in her words. She fears I'm drifting down a dark road, and she's sorry for me. I want to sink lower in my chair and cover my face with my book.

Rothbart looks at her and says, "You never say what you think."

Odette looks from Rothbart to me and back. Our father doesn't usually comment on our lives, but this

75

feels like an omen. Odette puzzles him out. He glances at me and returns to his book. His hand rests on the table next to a vial of some sick-smelling liquid, and we are all hushed.

She smiles at him and lovingly pours him a drink. Her gesture of kindness is like a warm fire in the middle of January. She doesn't complain or ask him to make things right. She would have said this was her way of putting him before her, just as she intends to put Prince Siegfried before her the rest of her days. Only I can see the tremor in her hand.

27

When I go into the kingdom, I have a new aura. A hush falls over the street. A cartwright gets a whisper of my presence and mutters to his son, "Go inside, now," without reason, but also without urgency. Instinct alone tells him to be afraid. In the whites of their eyes I begin to understand they don't see me as I am or as I see myself. They see a sinister, winged-like shadow, dark and looming. They know who I am, the sorceress of the lake, a midnight threat, the living parable they point to and whisper, "Like *her.*"

Their stories make me flat, and no one calls me by name. Witch, sorceress, necromancer, sprite. They don't call me what I am, Odile. Perhaps it hasn't dawned on them that I'm a person, too, and words hold power over me.

They expect me to come with fire and plague, to turn them into animals and make a show of storm and blood. But my magic is quiet. I mean to heal. In the tight, ungiving earth, healthy crops take root. During hunting parties, deer find their way out of harm. Even the sick son of a dairy farmer rises out of bed. Soon he's seen helping his father build a fence to pen the cows.

My work might amount to very little, yet they see storms. They see childless parents and sick neighbors and say, "The sorceress." I'm not surprised they twist the truth. To them I'm a brooding woman who clings to her resentment, and they invent lessons about my deeds to put into their tales. Their gossip has more to do with their pride than with any personal grudge against me. They need a scapegoat, someone to point to for the problems in their lives, and I embody for them all that is strange and other. They can't place me. I'm eccentric, a woman who defines herself, and they find this monstrous. So when storms fall upon the city, they go inside and tell more tales.

28

Sometimes when Prince Siegfried speaks, Odette looks far away, lost in thought. He would explain some courtly matter, and she wouldn't show her sadness. She keeps that to herself. Then he mentions the dawn and grabs his satchel and crossbow, and Odette smiles.

"Yes, it's time," she says.

I watch her the moments right after he leaves. She stares at the tall grasses, still swaying in his path. It's only a moment before the sun reaches for her. Her hair blows in the windless day, and in her place is a swan.

These are her most vulnerable moments, and these moments also she comes closest to being herself. Her future is everything to her now. She holds her fragile dream closely. When she awakes, unaware that she is being watched, she sobs, and I lower my gaze. When I see her again, soon before sunrise, she smiles and asks how I slept, her voice cheerful and almost song-like.

79

Too soon the sun shines, and I let the subject drop,
cowardly, and look away when her bright smile warps
in the daylight.

29

Resolve grows in me like a tumor, yet my heart breaks at the thought of forever losing my sister. I'm not certain what will become of me after the ball. Would the spell lash back like a sling shot, or would it taper off quietly? When the thing is done, would I crawl off into the woods, beneath the shadow of some oak, and breathe my last? I was sure of only one thing. After that night the two of us would not continue.

I soften when I see Odette again. "Will you be all right tonight?"

"Yes," she says.

"Can I get you anything?"

"No, thank you."

We sit on the bank tracing the star-swan Cygnus with our gaze, uncertain of each other.

I say, "He really likes you, doesn't he?"

"Yes." She looks at me. "Odile, these are the first of last times."

I look carefully at her, doubting myself, wondering if their love is more real than any stroke of magic. I could believe it when I see the way he looks at her, as if it's the last time and this were his way of saying, *Goodbye. I love you.*

"Yes," I echo. "The first of last times."

30

One night when Siegfried comes, I confuse his path, shifting roots and trees, leading him deep into the woods where I lie hidden.

I hear his footsteps and know he's close. He comes searching for Odette, unaware of the trees moving silently around him, searching perhaps for reassurance, for some honeyed words to ease the doubt growing in his mind that she'll come to the ball. Far off, Odette wades in the water, her eyes fixed on the night sky. There's disaster in the stars, and she feels it.

Siegfried's step changes. Slower now, perhaps he senses something threatening nearby. Perhaps he knows he's not welcome here. His step is halting, as if his heart is telling him to go the other way. I wrap my fingers around a branch and draw him farther and farther away from Odette.

The crossbow clicks and jostles on his back. He mutters to himself or to a counselor he imagines or to the shadows that swirl around him. This is my territory. The rules of the throne room, of laws written by people of his kind, won't protect him here. He is no more than a body muscling its way through the thicket, here on the starved edge of the world.

He pants as he wrestles with the bramble. I've drawn him to the deep of the forest where the pine needles bristle in the sky like the back of some monstrous creature. The moon shines brighter in this darkness than sunlight at high noon.

I hear the snap and shuffle of his arrival. The branch I'm grasping splinters in my grip. He's before me now, and I smile at my nerves. I can tell by the tightness of his brow that he senses magic all around him. He stops and takes his crossbow in hand, his finger on the trigger. In this cramped corner, bent as he is by the low-reaching branches, his weapon will do him no good.

"Who's there?" he says. He's near enough to see me, but my head is hooded and obscured by branches.

Then he sees my light hair cascading out of my mantle and says, overjoyed, "Odette!"

He sizes up the thick foliage around me. "Are you stuck? Can I get you out?" He comes closer and freezes. Something deeper than instinct tells him I'm not Odette.

I see the contour of his thought. He straightens and relaxes. He isn't as afraid of the sorceress as he thought he would be. His counselors and teachers have exaggerated how threatening my presence is.

"I know who you are," he says.

"Do you?"

"What are you planning to do with Odette?"

"Odette is gone. You have taken her away from me." My voice shakes.

"What have you done with her?"

I pull my mantle tightly around me and say slowly, "You think you honor and respect her, but what you take for love is your vanity. I don't think you know what it's like for her to be a swan. She's spared you from her burdens, Your Highness."

He seems to consider this. I say, "Do you want to know what she looks like in her honest moments?"

I lower my hood. My head shows bare through the branches.

"This, *this* is Odette."

He shifts his weight, unsure of himself.

"You thought Odette was a revelation. She is. I'm that revelation. You look for Odette, but you can't stand the sight of Odile. But she's always been here."

"Stop! I don't believe it. You can't be Odette."

"You don't know what she looks like in her true form."

"Liar!" he cries. His crossbow catches on a branch. He tries to yank it free.

"Know this, Prince," I say, backing away. "I will be at the ball."

Before he frees his crossbow, I am gone, bounding toward the tower.

Odette has gone to sleep. Her disappointment is like a blow in the gut, yet she breathes evenly and soon falls asleep.

Storm clouds gather around the city, and the leaves shudder in the wind.

31

In the throne room hang paintings of kings and queens who have gone before. They display their manifest nobility in gold and violet robes and ruby rings. The edges of their shoes are garnished with embroidery.

I sneak into the dimly lit room and study the expressions on the queens' faces. They look like they're holding something back. I hold my breath, listening closely, and sense a restlessness in the soft, umber shadows around them. I wonder about the oaths they took when they became queens. I approach them hesitantly. They smile enigmatically, like sphinxes, aware they have a certain mystery about them. I don't think Prince Siegfried really sees them when he's in the throne room. Instead, he sees the collective force of his legacy.

He holds counsel here, pacing in front of the paintings. He speaks of his plans to expand the kingdom, but without heart. He sounds like a schoolboy rehashing lines from a lexicon. Even his mother seems to falter in her confidence in him.

A counselor nods and takes notes. He and the others wish the best for their future king. The self-confident ones—Benno and several knights—don't pick up on their leader's lack of conviction.

Siegfried looks up, and though he can't see me in my dark corner, he fidgets under my scrutiny. He feels a little foolish for his plans, as if he knows I'm looking right through them.

I lower my gaze, and he blinks at last.

The conversation turns to me.

Someone asks, "Do you know what the sorceress is planning?"

The question is met with silence. Their steps sound softly in the room, and they face the question like they would face me, alarmed and unsure of themselves.

"She's coming to the ball," Siegfried says at last.

A hush falls over the room.

Benno says, "Then let her come. This may be our chance to move in on her."

Siegfried is faraway in his thoughts. I resist the urge

to set fire to Benno's shoes.

"If she wants to present herself in her true form, we can't be too careful," a counselor says, nodding at Benno.

Siegfried steps apart from them and gazes at the paintings of his ancestors. Only I hear him whisper, "What have you done to her?" All of a sudden, I pity him, half-wishing I wasn't so harsh with him the other night. I was angry, but I was also trying to prepare him for the coming heartache. I wish I could give him that settled place he searches for.

The others continue talking.

"No good, no good," Benno says, pacing and shaking his head darkly. "We don't know how powerful she is. We need to be ready for anything."

"Mm," the queen agrees. "Sorcery is bad business. She could turn us all wild. We'll be clucking chickens and won't know who we are anymore."

"But we can hope for a future with no darkness," another counselor says. "We can be prepared now that we know she's coming."

I've heard enough and leave them to their scheming. With a final look I see Benno rubbing his hands. The queen shakes her head at a counselor's remark, and

Siegfried stands lost in himself, his heart unmoored. He glances over his shoulder, shrinking under the gaze of his ancestors.

32

Not long after, angry at their plans, I tack a black cloth on each of the portraits, over the heads of their queens.

The queen screams when she sees them, and Siegfried turns white. There is no question of who did it, and at first the queen orders no one to touch them. She's afraid of my fury. Now, when she walks through the throne room and her faceless ancestors work on her like whispering spirits, she quickens her step.

33

Rain falls with increasing venom through the trees. The spires are shrouded in fog, and the world this night is cold and grey. The bloom, the freshness is greyed out. A woman emerges from her backdoor and scrapes the mud off her boots. She stirs at the sound of my footstep and narrows her eyes at the shadows moving in the dark. The storm clouds know she's eaten by some secret sorrow. A guardedness in her manner tells me she would go away if I made myself known. When she's back inside, I gather a bowl of wild berries and place it on her doorstep. She will thank her household gods, I know. She will consider herself blessed.

I inhale the smell of pine. I can't get away from that dark lady, Odile. I watch how the light falls on the swan's feathers and listen to the echo of cones falling off trees. The wood-sounds of the forest shift, and I pause to listen to the growing thrum. It may be that only in slaying the swan will I be free of her at last.

34

As the ball approaches, noble ladies come from distant kingdoms and stay in the castle. They believe the prince still needs a bride. Their clothing—gold velvets and crimson silks, floral embroidery, tall hats with sweeping veils—creates a force of beauty that dazzles me. In days before, I would have wanted to be their trusted handmaiden and confidante. In search of satin slippers, I would feel more beautiful in the halo of such elegance.

Their futures have been laid out for them like choreography. They can't define themselves, and what they see in the mirror is what they think the prince wants to see.

Some days I imagine we could be friends, if my circumstances were different, if my animal nature didn't loom between us, displacing me from ordinary society by miles.

In another room, the fire in the hearth blazes, and the prince's eyes flash in the warm light. Perhaps he's coming to believe that if Odette isn't real, then there is no bride for him. I watch him, but when he lifts his eyes in my direction, I disappear before his sadness makes me fall at his feet and tell him I'll be whoever he wants me to be if only he would be happy.

Upstairs in the guest rooms, the ladies lie down to rest, and resolve grows inside of me like wisteria.

35

The ball is days away now. Rather than spying on the kingdom, I would be wiser to lie low in the chilly, dark tower house reading and refining spells. It's safer in my own realm, sitting in the cool, blue shadows, my spells illuminated by flashes of firelight, and I, breathing the cloying air of the tower house, studying the slanting black ink in my book. Yet I still go to them. Outside, the reeds bow in the wind. The moon is half-lidded, dim. Clouds unfold delicately across the skies. I draw myself up, bound toward the castle.

The gate door lies open in the yawning night. A watchguard leans on the wall and hooks his hand on the chain. It shudders and creaks. In the distance comes the screeching of crickets, one louder than the rest. He doesn't realize the trembling from the chain isn't from his touch. The bell tolls, and for a moment he leaves his post.

I approach the orange light of the banquet hall. Inside, the queen and the rest of them are bending over their meat. The air is suffused with the smell of pig roast and mulled wine. Displayed on the table is a boar hunted by the prince himself. Their cutlery make sharp cast shadows in the torchlight. I feel for the cats who are hungry, sitting motionless on the windowsill.

I perch myself in a high window and watch the men lift their cups to Prince Siegfried. They've put their hopes in the ball, the event that will mean my downfall. They want the land purged of dark magic. The prince stares at the fire, his expression blank. If the kingdom really were in his hands, I believe he would make peace with me. They tell him to protect this house from unsightly beasts, and he has his duty to stand by.

Night deepens. The queen slouches, red-faced, and one woman acts drowsy and retires for the night. For a moment all goes quiet. The moon dips behind the clouds, and our shadows mingle, boundless.

Then Siegfried takes his crossbow and excuses himself.

When he's gone, Benno speaks to the room of silent, waiting people, rousing their sense of security.

"You don't have to be afraid. The sorcerer and his

daughter have been a threat to us, and we haven't known how to protect ourselves from them. But the ball will be a turning point. When the sorceress comes, she'll try to cast a spell on the prince, but we'll be ready to counter her attack."

He continues, "We won't be haunted by shadows much longer. We'll have new land to cultivate, new wood and stone to build with. Our struggle has been silent. We've gone on with courage, but if we paid attention, we'd feel darkness weighing on our hearts."

Benno pauses. The queen nods. She's pleased with this. At least someone's been paying attention. Very soon her kingdom would expand, and all those marshy woods would be put to use. No one in the room tempers the vision. The lords and ladies listen with bated breath, steam rising silently from their plates.

After some time, the doors swing open, and Siegfried appears, breathing heavily, his hands empty.

36

He says nothing, but his face is stricken. I shut my eyes and see him in the woods, clenching his crossbow as if it were the one thing he could hold on to in this world of passing visions and double faces. He moves like one caught without a light, feeling around with his hands, and yet he has faith he'll find Odette at the end of his searching.

At the bank of the lake, he comes upon my father, who's picking mushrooms and tossing them into a basket.

"Where is Odette?" Siegfried says, his desperation winning over his fear of Rothbart.

"You won't find her here."

"What have you done with her?"

Rothbart plucks a few mushrooms. He says, "Did she tell you yet she's a sorceress?"

Siegfried relaxes his grip on the crossbow. "Odile is the sorceress." His voice is uncertain.

Rothbart smiles. He continues to paw the soil for mushrooms, his nose casting a long shadow across his cheek. Without looking at the prince, he says, "You know that weapon won't do you any good here."

Siegfried looks at it. "Does magic protect you?"

"That's not what I meant. You could hurt me if you wanted to."

Siegfried studies him. He looks from his crossbow to the basket to Rothbart again. Then he does something that surprises them both. He lays the crossbow beside the basket of mushrooms.

Siegfried retreats from the bank, leaving Rothbart to stare at the weapon, absently rubbing a clump of dirt to a powder.

37

Back in the banquet hall, I open my eyes and watch Siegfried step weakly into the room. What the sorcerer said to him, what he saw that night when I showed my face, rush to his mind, and he staggers. He can't deny anymore what he's refused to believe.

Benno opens his mouth to make another speech but stops when Siegfried collapses into the seat next to him. Water puddles at the prince's feet from his wet boots.

Benno watches him. We are both watching him. Siegfried turns his pallid face toward me, and I lean in from the window, barely breathing.

The fire in the hearth grows dim, and Benno lays his hand on the prince's shoulder. I clutch at my chest. The hole widens inside of me as if I, too, have just come to believe that Odette is gone.

38

On the eve of the ball the guests go to bed one by one. The women take the pins out of their hair and massage their scalps, welcoming the release. They would sleep on their backs and pray for gravity to pull their skin smooth.

Water drips on a leaf, regimented. I walk past the agitated ferns and climb the mass of boulders that juts into the lake. If Odette were here, she would observe the clumps of shy grass that grow out of the rocky crevices. Up here, there is only a step between the jagged ledge and the water below. All is quiet except for the steady raindrops and the lapping of waves. A frog croaks. A dark shadow passes through the water. My mantle billows in the icy wind.

Then Odette comes, she to whom all my thoughts fly. She walks on the water, moving toward me. Her feet are just covered in the frothy waves. Her flaxen hair gleams from a bright light in the tower.

I say, stupidly, "You're here?"

I'm on edge. I want to make her tell me everything—how we are the same and yet different, how the prince could have visited her all those nights, what will happen when I deceive him at the ball tomorrow. These thoughts converge at once, and I become tongue-tied.

At last I find my voice. "What have you been doing all this time?"

I've been waiting for the right moment to talk to you.

"Waiting?" She doesn't elaborate. "Have you seen Prince Siegfried?" I cringe at the mention of his name. If she knew I'm about to break his heart even more, she might disappear in the starlight, not wanting to talk to me at all.

Sometimes, from far away. Odile, I need to speak to you. I know you're planning to go to the ball in my place.

I try to read her expression. I say nervously, "Well, what about it?"

Don't you see Siegfried is on your side, or would be if you'd let him be? You've made up your mind what he's about, but you've never bothered to understand him. All those times he visited, he was waiting for me to tell him about my life—about father, the curse, living like an exile outside his kingdom. I know he wanted to ask about it, but I kept it all to myself. He was waiting for me to tell him in my own timing. And I knew all along he couldn't wait for that day.

I laugh, sounding more scornful than I mean to. I don't like the sound of any of this. I'm the one who's been misunderstood, and it stings to hear I've willfully misunderstood him.

She's close enough to touch, she down on the water and I on the precipice. I take a step toward her.

Let it go, Odile. You're trying so hard to take everything into your own hands, but you can't do it on your own. Don't steal his vow from him.

"But what about the curse? Don't you think I should end this crazy dream I'm having?" My voice rises to a shout. "Look at you. You're not even real. Why am I even talking to you? You're walking on *water*."

The wind picks up. Across the way, Father emerges from the wood, scowling at the storm clouds and looking wet and soggy. He stops short when he sees me through the rain.

He calls out, "Odile, get down from there." He clambers up a boulder and waves both arms at me, his mantle flapping loudly in the wind.

In my fury I ignore him. I will have the last word with Odette.

"You're just saying this because you're jealous I'm going to the ball and you aren't. Let me tell you something. After the ball, you're never going to appear again!"

Fine. For the first time, an edge creeps into her voice.

She turns away and begins to sink into the water.

"Wait. Wait!" I howl, eyes wild, reaching for her.

She sinks fully into the water. Soon only her hair mingles with the reflected starlight, and then she's gone.

I blink. The import of her words slowly begins to weigh on me, and I lose my balance. A shout sounds through the storm, and I feel myself being yanked back. I focus my attention and become aware of my father, holding my arm. His face is half relieved, half annoyed. I glance back and realize I was about to fall into the lake.

I say, "Did you see her, too?"

He shakes his head, but he puts his arm around me and holds me closely, his gaze fixed on the spot where she disappeared.

39

The next morning I awake from a deep slumber. I rub my eyes groggily and watch the room slowly come into focus—a pile of books on my chair, my wooden wardrobe, my mantle hanging from the wall. Then, as if it just happened, my encounter with Odette comes rushing back to me. I sit up in bed.

Whether or not it was a dream, I may never know. She's a voice, I tell myself, merely a voice inside my head. I throw my blanket back and get ready for the day.

It would be easy to stay home from the ball tonight. I'm comfortable at home, but that would be the greatest betrayal of myself. I could never be rid of my curse that way. This is the decision that would make a true sorceress of me or prove that all along I've been a nightmare walking.

I haven't told him, but Rothbart knows I'm going.

I find him asleep on the floor of his study. I put a pillow under his head and throw a woolen blanket over him.

He mutters something and rolls over. He might want to go to the ball himself and give the court a piece of his mind, but he's so tired. Odette isn't the only one who's been worn out by the spell. If he reflected on it, he might realize he's torn between the anger he feels toward the court and the anger he feels toward himself.

I leave him, letting the blanket subdue his dreams.

40

I ron grey storm clouds gather round the spires. I walk purposefully toward the castle, set in motion like a cannonball. Above me the swan courses through the air. When this is over, when I've come and gone from their ballroom like a dark storm cloud, I will meet her at the lake. Her wings glimmer in the atmosphere, and I quicken my step.

Somewhere deep in the castle, Siegfried stands waiting like granite. He doesn't know how the night will end. Glancing at the swan once more, I couldn't be sure, either.

41

The streets are still as deep waters. There is no sound but the creak of an old hinge as a shudder swings loose. Crossing the front grounds of the castle, the hedges rising on either side of me, eerie shapes in the darkness, I hear a music coming from the ballroom. The turrets of the castle stand out against the blue-green sky, like black cut paper. The breeze lifts. I remember one night staying up late with Odette, sitting on a sloping hill off the causeway and looking at the castle like we were two stars bending their light on the city. Our father soared across the half-lidded moon, like a dragon, his leathery wings flapping in the dewy night. I feel like a specter, with no earthly substance. The music slows down, and the turrets seem to lean in, listening with every stone. In this moment I sense my age, that first deception, years that unfolded in stillness.

My heart pounds, and I step into the bustling hall with a clarity of purpose I have rarely known.

Prowling around the edges of the room are Benno's guards, a dozen or more. Benno spots me and gives the signal for them to move in. They do by degrees, not wanting to cause a stir.

I scan the room for the prince. He stands in the center of the room, his face grey and hollow.

As I make my way across the flagstone floor and the guards come closer, more and more guests become aware of me. The queen frowns and rises from her seat. Around me noblewomen gather in small groups. They are tall and striking in their high hats, and their dresses create a mosaic of red and purple and yellow fabrics. I hear the words, "That can't be the sorceress. She looks scared."

At last I'm in the center of the room, face-to-face with Prince Siegfried. I do what Odette could never have done, nor Rothbart nor I in my nobler moments. I incant a spell over the prince. He shuts his eyes, and when he opens them, he looks at me overjoyed, thinking I'm Odette.

"Odette," he says. "You're really here!"

He laughs and swirls me around. His heart brims with love, and his face beams as if all the light in the room is gathered within him.

"Don't cry," he says. "You're here now. It's going to be all right."

The lump in my throat swells painfully. I cannot speak. Such tender words have never felt like daggers. This is my ultimate betrayal of him and of that better part of me that is Odette.

He says, "Odette, will you marry me?"

The music comes to an inharmonious stop. The queen and Benno watch, baffled.

I nod. The spell swells in my chest. I grab onto his hand with both of mine, like a drowning woman grasping at a rope. "Promise," I say hoarsely, waiting for the word that would unshackle me forever.

"Odette, I vow to love you and cherish you for as long as I live, my queen and dearest friend."

His mother, in spite of herself, dabs her eyes with a handkerchief. Benno stares at us.

I feel an ice-hot tingling all over my body. I have no time to think but quickly cause the lights of the torches and the hearth to go out. Even the windows shut out the moon and the stars, and soon we are in utter darkness. A few people scream, and confusion reigns throughout the room.

Benno shouts, "It's a trick! Stop that woman!"

His troops jostle against one another and bump against furniture in their haste.

I hear the prince say, "It can't be." The delusion passed, and he realizes he wasn't speaking to Odette.

"I'm sorry," I whisper, and I hope with every fiber of my being that one day he will forgive me. "This was the only way I knew how to break my curse."

I let go of him. He gropes in the darkness, "Wait. *Wait*! Don't leave!"

Benno shouts for a light. A few servants fumble with some kindling, but each flame they start goes out with a flicker.

"Run for your lives!" the queen shrieks. "She's going to turn us all into chickens!"

At last Benno gets hold of a lighted torch and sweeps it around him looking for me. He's as angry as a bull. For all his preparation, I slipped from his fingers, and his glory was snatched from beneath his nose. Soon the hearth roars again with a fire, and the celestial lights shine through the windows.

But by then I am gone.

42

The causeway seems to grow longer as I rush home, or perhaps I move more heavily with my grief. The wind howls with the coming storm. At last I am at the lake, panting with weariness. I blink at the oak trees and realize I am the one who made these woods fearsome, and in my mind alone have they ever held such fear. I look around and see the swan floating on the lake.

The water gleams in the moonlight. I look from the castle to the lake, my eyes stinging with tears. Though I have stood here countless times, tonight I do not recognize this place. Like Odette and the swan nightmare I've been living, I might have made it all up.

One thing remains.

"I will no longer be Odette," I bawl, swollen-eyed and scowling at the swan. My eyes fall on the crossbow, still where the prince left it. The swan watches me as I lift it, heavy, unwieldy weapon that it is. "This will be your greatest achievement," I mutter to it. "You're going to release me from her at last."

I hold it clumsily at my shoulder and aim at the swan. I will probably miss, and the realization makes me laugh, harder than the situation seems to call for. Then all at once I am calm and cold, I begin to pull the trigger.

"Don't, please!"

Startled, I nearly drop the crossbow. The voice is Prince Siegfried's, but my mind has trouble making sense of his presence here. I might have awakened from a vivid dream only to find myself in a strange room, squinting at the walls and furniture that were not my own.

But there he is, leaning with his hand on a tree. He must have sprinted here because he's still catching his breath.

"If you pull that trigger, you will bring yourself harm," he says between breaths.

I turn slowly toward him, hardly daring to believe he's here.

"I still mean every word I said," he says, and already he's prying the weapon out of my hands. "I mean them for you."

I look down and my hands are in his. I feel the last surge of enchantment grow faint, and I no longer feel the spark that caused fire and rain. I look over, and the swan has vanished. I know instinctively she has escaped to a place I never believed existed, a settled place, a place of rest.

Last of all I look at Siegfried, who says my name softly.

The End

About The Author

Anna Tipton was born and raised in Northwest Indiana and studied at Wheaton College.

She currently lives in the greater Chicago area and Naples, Florida.

ACKNOWLEDGEMENTS

I'm very grateful to the people who helped me while I worked on this piece.

For the amazing team at Hidden Shelf, especially for Bob Gaines, who believed in it and shepherded it to the version it is today, and for Megan Whitfield, Kerstin Stokes, and Rachel Wickstrom.

For Abbie Pettit, who read numerous drafts and generously shared her feedback, ideas, and encouragement.

For Trudy Hale of the Porches; Courtney Sexton and Rachel Coonce of The Inner Loop; and the good people of the Woodlawn Estate, Pope-Leighey House, and Arcadia Center. Their writing residencies provided valuable time and space for me to work.

For Cammy, Jessie, and Mariah, who stood by me from the beginning.

And as always, for my family.

The cover art for *Swan Vanishing* from internationally acclaimed artist Megan Whitfield was featured during the Maryland Federation of Art's 2022 Spring Member Show.

Anna Tipton

Explore the Hidden Shelf

117